Mafia Love: A Captive Heart

Mrigendra Bharti

Published by Sellbrochure Vymish Entertainment, 2024.

This is a work of fiction. Similarities to real people, places, or events are entirely coincidental.

MAFIA LOVE: A CAPTIVE HEART

First edition. October 4, 2024.

Copyright © 2024 Mrigendra Bharti.

ISBN: 979-8227787064

Written by Mrigendra Bharti.

Table of Contents

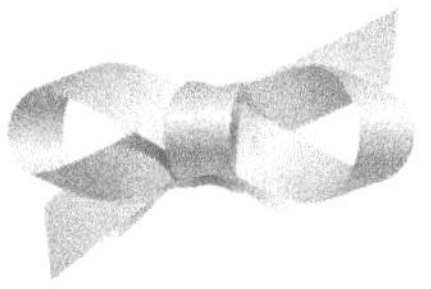

Preface

IN A WORLD WHERE LOVE often encounters obstacles, Mafia Love: A Captive Heart delves into the depths of passion and the lengths one might go to protect it. This story is a testament to the power of love, the strength of resolve, and the unbreakable bonds that can form in the most unexpected circumstances.

Set against the backdrop of a bustling city and the innocence of school days, the tale follows Mahir and Avni, two young souls whose hearts intertwine during their final moments in school. Their connection is immediate, filled with the sweetness of youthful dreams and the promise of a bright future. But as their love blossoms, so do the challenges they face. Avni's family, bound by tradition and expectations, disapproves of their union, leaving Mahir desperate to prove his worth and devotion.

As the pressure mounts, Mahir finds himself at a crossroads, grappling with the desperation of unrequited love and the fear of losing the girl who has captured his heart. What follows is a daring journey into the underbelly of passion, where Mahir adopts a dangerous persona to seize control of his fate. In a bold move, he kidnaps Avni, transforming their love story into a thrilling ride filled with suspense, emotion, and unexpected twists.

This book is more than just a love story; it is a reflection of the complexities of relationships, the clash between tradition and modernity, and the fierce determination to follow one's heart. It explores the idea that love, in its purest form, can transcend barriers and redefine the very meaning of commitment.

As you embark on this journey with Mahir and Avni, prepare to experience the exhilaration of their adventures, the tenderness of their connection, and the trials that test their love. It is my hope that you will find yourself immersed in their world, feeling every heartbeat and breath as they navigate the chaos of their emotions.

Welcome to Mafia Love: A Captive Heart, where love knows no bounds, and every moment is a testament to the lengths we will go for those we hold dear.

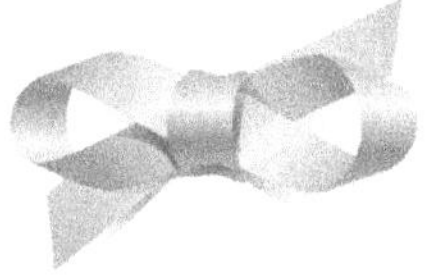

Prologue

THE AIR WAS THICK WITH anticipation, charged with the laughter and chatter of students relishing their last days of school. The sun dipped low, casting a warm golden glow over the campus, illuminating the faces of young dreamers about to embark on their next adventures. Among them was Mahir, a boy with ambitions larger than life and a heart that beat only for one—Avni.

From the moment he had first laid eyes on her, there was an unexplainable spark, a connection that pulled him toward her like gravity. Avni, with her contagious laughter and radiant smile, had unwittingly carved a place in his heart, igniting a flame he had never known existed. As days turned into months, their friendship blossomed into something deeper, filled with stolen glances and unspoken words.

But as their school days drew to a close, the shadows of reality loomed over their idyllic world. Avni's family had plans for her—a future that didn't include Mahir. As whispers of an arranged marriage began to circulate, Mahir's heart sank, the walls of his dream collapsing around him. Desperation took root, and with it came an undeniable determination to change their fate.

In the quiet corners of his mind, a dangerous idea began to take shape. He envisioned a life where love triumphed over all, a life where he could hold Avni close, free from the chains of societal expectations. Little did he know that his journey would take a perilous turn, leading him down a path he had never imagined.

As the last bell rang and students flooded out of the gates, Mahir knew one thing for certain: he would not let Avni slip away without a fight. Their love story was just beginning, and he was willing to do whatever it took to keep her in his life—even if it meant becoming something he never thought he would be.

This is a tale of love that defies the ordinary, a story that dances on the edge of danger, where a boy's heart leads him to become a force to be reckoned with—a story of Mafia Love: A Captive Heart.

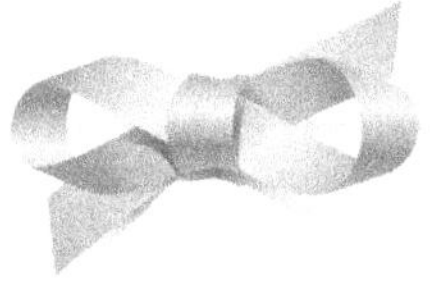

About Sellbrochure IPDP

SELLBROCHURE VYMISH Entertainment, recognized as India's largest book publishing company, has made significant strides in ensuring its extensive collection of books reaches audiences across the global market. This rapid expansion is a testament to the company's dedication to disseminating knowledge and literature far beyond national borders. Central to its success is its affiliation with InkWhirl Media Networks, a reputable entity in the media and publication industry known for its innovative and strategic approaches. Within this network, InkWhirl Publication LLC operates as a vital division, further enhancing the company's capabilities and reach in the international market.

The visionary behind this enterprise is Mrigendra Bharti, the founder of Sellbrochure Vymish Entertainment. His foresight and passion for the literary world have been instrumental in steering the company towards remarkable growth and recognition. Under his leadership, Sellbrochure Vymish Entertainment has not only expanded its catalog but also established a strong presence in both domestic and international markets. Mrigendra Bharti's commitment to excellence and innovation has been a driving force in the company's journey, ensuring that it stays ahead of industry trends and meets the evolving needs of readers worldwide.

Sellbrochure Vymish Entertainment operates under the robust support of its parental organization, Mrigendra Bharti Group InfoTech. This affiliation provides the necessary resources and strategic guidance, enabling the publishing company to undertake ambitious projects and explore new markets. Mrigendra Bharti Group InfoTech's extensive experience in technology and information services has been a valuable asset, allowing Sellbrochure Vymish Entertainment to integrate advanced digital solutions in its operations, thereby enhancing its distribution capabilities and reader engagement.

Through relentless efforts and a commitment to quality, Sellbrochure Vymish Entertainment continues to break barriers and expand the reach of Indian literature globally. The company's diverse portfolio includes a wide range of genres, catering to different age groups and interests, thereby fostering a rich and inclusive reading culture. As it continues to innovate and grow, Sellbrochure Vymish Entertainment remains dedicated to its mission of making literature accessible to all, contributing significantly to the global literary landscape.

Connect With Mrigendra,
Thank you very much for choosing this book.
You can also connect with me on Instagram,
https://www.instagram.com/i_mrigendrabharti.official
With Love,
Mrigendra Bharti

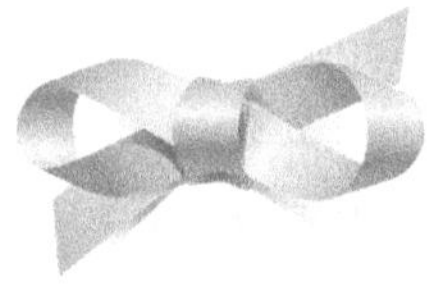

Introduction

WELCOME TO MAFIA LOVE: A Captive Heart, a tale where the boundaries of love are tested and redefined in ways one might never expect. In this captivating story, we journey through the lives of Mahir and Avni, two young souls whose innocent connection during their school years blossoms into a passionate love that faces insurmountable challenges.

Set against the backdrop of a vibrant school life, their story unfolds as they navigate the excitement of friendship, the sweetness of first love, and the heart-wrenching reality of societal expectations. As they prepare to say goodbye to their school days, the stakes rise when Avni's family reveals plans for an arranged marriage, leaving Mahir desperate to hold onto the girl who has captured his heart.

What begins as a simple crush evolves into a fierce love that ignites Mahir's determination to prove his worth and secure their future together. However, when words fail and circumstances grow dire, Mahir takes a drastic step that propels them both into a world of uncertainty and danger. In his quest for love, he adopts a persona that embodies strength and rebellion, transforming from an ordinary boy into a figure of intrigue and power.

Mafia Love: A Captive Heart is more than just a romantic escapade; it delves into themes of loyalty, sacrifice, and the lengths one will go to protect what they cherish. As Mahir and

Avni's story unfolds, readers will witness their struggles and triumphs, exploring the complexities of love in a world that often imposes its own rules.

Through moments of passion, tension, and heartache, this narrative invites you to experience the intensity of young love and the transformative power it holds. Join Mahir and Avni on their journey as they discover that true love is not only about finding each other but also about fighting for a future against all odds.

Prepare yourself for an unforgettable adventure filled with emotions that will resonate long after the final page. Welcome to a world where love can be both beautiful and dangerous—a world where hearts can be captured, lost, and ultimately freed.

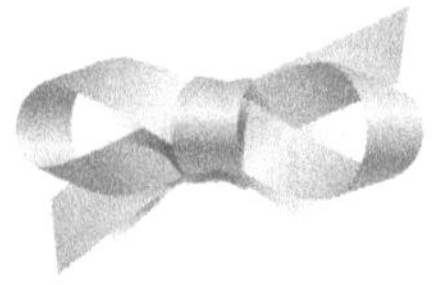

Chapter 1 The Last Day of School

First Meet up

THE LAST DAY OF SCHOOL always carried a bittersweet feeling. The familiar corridors, the classrooms that once echoed with laughter, and the friends that you've spent years with—all of it seemed to pass by like a blur. Mahir stood by the window of his classroom, his eyes lost in the horizon, thinking about how these moments would soon become memories.

He sighed, his thoughts consumed by the ending of this chapter of life. Yet, somewhere in the corner of his heart, there was an unspoken excitement, a strange anticipation. He didn't know why, but today felt different.

Just then, the classroom door creaked open, and in walked Avni. She was like a breath of fresh air—simple yet captivating. Her long black hair swayed with each step, and her doe-like eyes scanned the room nervously, as if she were searching for something—or someone.

Mahir had seen Avni before, but never this closely. They were in the same batch, but their paths had never really crossed. She was the quiet type, always immersed in her own world, while Mahir was more of an extrovert, always surrounded by friends. But today, as their eyes met, something shifted.

Mahir's heart skipped a beat. For a second, everything around him blurred. It was as if the noise of the bustling classroom had faded, leaving just the two of them in this silent, shared moment. He had never felt this way before—not with anyone. He watched as she nervously tucked a strand of hair behind her ear, her gaze meeting his for just a brief second before she looked away, shyly.

"What just happened?" Mahir muttered under his breath, his pulse quickening. He felt a wave of emotions surge through him, emotions he couldn't quite put into words.

He turned to his friend Rohit, sitting beside him. "Who is she?" Mahir asked, his voice filled with curiosity.

Rohit chuckled. "That's Avni. You don't know her? She's in our batch, man."

"I know that," Mahir replied, unable to take his eyes off her. "But I mean... I've never really noticed her before."

Rohit grinned, sensing Mahir's newfound interest. "Well, she's always been around, just a little quiet. Why? Thinking of talking to her now that it's the last day?"

Mahir smirked slightly, but deep inside, he felt an unexplainable pull. There was something about Avni that was different. She wasn't just another classmate. He had no idea what it was, but he was determined to find out.

As the final bell rang, signaling the end of their school years, the classroom filled with chatter and excitement. Everyone was busy exchanging goodbyes, promising to stay in touch, and making plans for the future. But Mahir's eyes were locked on Avni as she gathered her books and slowly made her way toward the door.

Without thinking twice, Mahir followed her out into the corridor. His heart raced, not knowing what he would say or how she would respond, but he knew he had to talk to her.

"Avni?" he called out, his voice softer than usual.

She turned around, her eyes widening a little in surprise. "Mahir, right?"

He nodded, feeling a strange sense of relief that she knew his name. "Yeah, I... I just wanted to say hi. It's our last day, and... well, I don't think we've ever really talked."

Avni smiled, a small but warm smile that made his heart flutter. "I guess not. It's funny, isn't it? We've been in the same class for years, but somehow never crossed paths."

Mahir chuckled nervously. "Yeah, funny. I mean, I've seen you around, but... I never realized how—" He stopped himself before blurting out something too forward. "I mean, I guess I never realized how nice it would be to actually talk to you."

Avni raised an eyebrow, amused. "Well, I'm glad you did now."

There was an awkward silence for a moment, but it wasn't uncomfortable. It was as if both of them were unsure of what to say next, but they didn't mind just being there, in that shared space, even if only for a few moments.

"So... what are your plans now? After school, I mean," Mahir asked, trying to keep the conversation going.

"I'm not sure yet," Avni replied, tucking a loose strand of hair behind her ear. "Maybe college, maybe something else. What about you?"

"I think college, too," Mahir said. "But, to be honest, I haven't really thought that far ahead. It all feels so... overwhelming."

Avni nodded in agreement. "Yeah, it does. It's like, we've been in this comfortable routine for years, and now... everything's about to change."

They both stood there for a while, letting the weight of those words sink in. The future felt uncertain, but in that moment, Mahir didn't care. All he could think about was how much he wanted to know more about her, how much he wanted to stay in this moment just a little longer.

"Listen," Mahir finally said, breaking the silence. "I know it's the last day and all, but... would you like to maybe grab a coffee sometime? I mean, if you're free or... if you'd want to."

Avni looked at him, her eyes sparkling with a hint of surprise. "Coffee?"

"Yeah," Mahir said, trying to play it cool. "You know, just to... talk. Get to know each other. No pressure."

She smiled again, this time a little wider. "I'd like that."

Mahir felt his heart soar. "Really?"

"Yeah," Avni replied softly. "I mean, it's not every day you make a new friend on your last day of school, right?"

He chuckled, feeling a warmth spread through him. "Right. So... I'll see you soon then?"

"See you soon, Mahir," she said, giving him a small wave before turning to leave.

As Mahir watched her walk away, he couldn't help but smile. Something had changed in that brief interaction, and he had a feeling it was just the beginning of something beautiful. For the first time in a long while, the future didn't seem so uncertain anymore.

It seemed full of possibilities.

And at the center of it all was Avni.

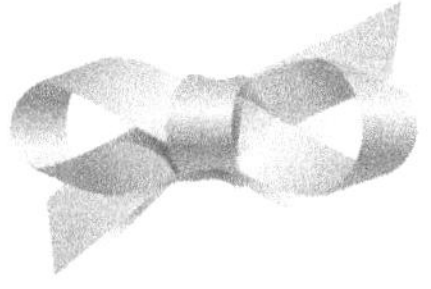

A New Beginning

MAHIR COULDN'T STOP thinking about his conversation with Avni. As he walked back home, her smile kept playing in his mind like a sweet melody. The simplicity of their talk, the ease with which they connected, felt so natural, yet so different from any other interaction he had ever had.

By the time Mahir reached home, the sun was setting, casting a golden glow over everything. He slumped onto his bed, staring at the ceiling, and wondered what it was about Avni that made her stand out. Sure, she was beautiful—her delicate features, her graceful way of moving—but there was something deeper. It was the way she seemed genuinely interested, the way her eyes sparkled when she spoke, the way her smile felt so... real.

For the next few days, Mahir found himself anxiously waiting to see her again. They had exchanged numbers before parting ways, and every time his phone buzzed, his heart leaped a little. He wanted to text her, but at the same time, he didn't want to come off as too eager.

"What do I even say?" he thought to himself, scrolling through their brief chat history. Avni had simply texted him the word "Hi" the night they met, and he had replied with a casual "Hey :)". That was it—no follow-up conversation, no continuation.

Days passed, and although they hadn't spoken much, Mahir couldn't shake off the thought of her. On one particularly warm evening, as he sat in a café sipping on a cold coffee, he decided he couldn't wait any longer. Mahir unlocked his phone, opened their chat, and started typing:

Mahir: Hey, Avni! How have you been? :)

He paused, stared at the screen, then hit send. His heart raced as he placed his phone on the table, trying not to think about it too much. But it was no use. Every passing second felt like an eternity.

Just as he was about to give up hope, his phone buzzed.

Avni: Hey, Mahir! I've been good. How about you? :)

Mahir couldn't help but smile. The little emoji at the end of her message made his heart race. He quickly typed back:

Mahir: I'm good, too! I was just thinking about how it's only been a few days since school ended, but it already feels so different. Have you been up to anything?

Avni replied almost instantly:

Avni: I know, right? It feels weird not having to wake up early for school. I've mostly been relaxing, trying to figure out what to do next.

Mahir felt a sense of relief. Their conversation was flowing naturally, and he was beginning to feel more at ease.

Mahir: Yeah, it's like we suddenly have all this free time, but I have no idea what to do with it! Have you thought about college yet?

There was a slight pause before she responded.

Avni: Not really. I'm still deciding. My parents want me to go to a local college, but I'm thinking of taking a gap year. Just to explore a bit, you know?

Mahir: That sounds amazing! I've always wanted to take some time off and travel. Where would you go if you could?

Another pause. Mahir could almost imagine her thinking, her fingers hovering over her phone as she considered her answer.

Avni: I think I'd start with the mountains. There's something about the peace and quiet up there that calls to me.

Mahir smiled. He hadn't expected that answer, but it made sense. Avni seemed like someone who appreciated the simpler, quieter things in life.

Mahir: That sounds incredible. I've always wanted to visit the mountains, too. Maybe we'll run into each other up there someday. (⌒‿◇)

Avni's response came quickly, and it made Mahir's heart skip a beat.

Avni: Maybe we will. :)

There was something about the way their conversation flowed that felt effortless, like they had known each other for years rather than just a few brief moments in school. Mahir felt a sense of connection with Avni that he hadn't felt with anyone else before. It was strange, exciting, and a little terrifying.

Over the next few weeks, they continued to text each other, their conversations growing longer and more frequent. They talked about everything—school memories, their favorite movies, their dreams for the future. Each message brought them closer, and Mahir found himself looking forward to their chats more than anything else.

One evening, as they were texting, Avni suggested something unexpected:

Avni: Hey, what do you think about meeting up this weekend? I know a great café near my place. We could grab coffee, like we talked about.

Mahir's heart raced. The idea of seeing her again filled him with excitement, but also a bit of nervousness. What if things didn't go as smoothly in person as they did over text? What if he said something awkward?

But he couldn't resist the thought of seeing her again.

Mahir: I'd love that! Saturday, right? What time?

Avni: Let's say around 4 PM? I'll send you the address. :)

Mahir could barely contain his excitement. He spent the next few days imagining how the meetup would go, rehearsing what he would say, and trying to keep his nerves in check. He had never felt this way about anyone before, and the thought of spending more time with Avni made his heart flutter in a way he hadn't experienced before.

Finally, the day came. Mahir arrived at the café a little early, his heart pounding with anticipation. He checked his phone to see if Avni had texted, but there was nothing. Taking a deep breath, he decided to wait outside.

As he stood there, he saw her walking toward him. Avni looked just as he remembered—simple, elegant, with that same warm smile that had captivated him from the very beginning. She waved, her eyes bright with excitement.

"Hey!" she called out as she approached.

"Hey," Mahir replied, trying to keep his voice steady. "You look great."

Avni blushed slightly, tucking her hair behind her ear. "Thanks. You too."

They walked into the café together, the warm scent of coffee filling the air around them. As they sat down, Mahir felt a sense of calm wash over him. This felt right. Being here with Avni, talking to her in person, laughing over coffee—it was everything he had imagined and more.

The hours passed by quickly, and before they knew it, the sun was setting. As they walked out of the café, Avni looked at Mahir, a soft smile playing on her lips.

"This was fun," she said.

"Yeah, it was," Mahir agreed, his heart full. "We should do it again sometime."

Avni nodded. "I'd like that."

As they said their goodbyes and went their separate ways, Mahir couldn't help but feel that this was the start of something special.

Something real.

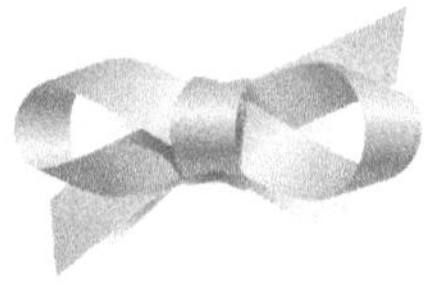

Chapter 2: Silent Confessions

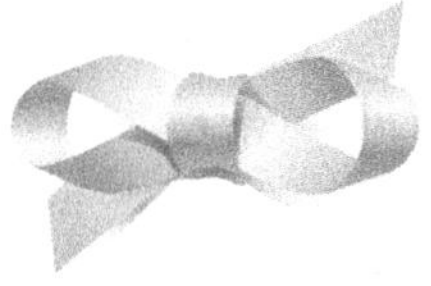

Unspoken Feelings

THE NEXT FEW DAYS AFTER their café meet-up were like a dream for Mahir. Every moment he spent talking to Avni, whether through texts or the occasional calls, made him feel closer to her. They were becoming more than just casual acquaintances. Every word, every laugh, every tiny detail they shared brought them deeper into each other's lives.

But with every growing connection, Mahir couldn't help but feel an undercurrent of something he couldn't quite name. There was a pull between them, a silent tension that made him wonder if Avni felt it too.

One evening, while sitting on his terrace, Mahir's phone buzzed. It was Avni. The notification alone made him smile. The conversations had become more frequent lately, and Mahir looked forward to them more than he'd like to admit.

Avni: Hey! What are you doing? :)

Mahir: Nothing much, just enjoying the breeze. What about you?

Avni: Same here! It's such a peaceful night, isn't it?

Mahir leaned back against the cool tiles, looking up at the sky. The stars seemed brighter than usual tonight, twinkling down like they were in on some secret. His fingers hovered over the keyboard as he typed back.

Mahir: Yeah, nights like this make you think about... everything.

There was a brief pause before Avni replied.

Avni: Everything? Like what?

Mahir hesitated. Should he tell her? Should he admit the thoughts swirling in his head, the ones that had been bothering him for days? He decided to keep it light—for now.

Mahir: You know, life... the future... stuff like that.

Avni didn't reply for a while, and Mahir wondered if he had said something wrong. But then, the phone buzzed again.

Avni: Do you ever think about... us?

Mahir's breath hitched as he reread the message. His fingers froze. Had she really just asked that? His heart raced, thoughts spinning in every direction. This was the moment he had been waiting for, but also the moment he feared.

Did Avni feel the same way about him? Or was she just asking as a friend?

Mahir: Sometimes... yeah. Do you?

There was a longer pause this time, and Mahir could feel his heart pounding in his chest. His mind raced with possibilities, each one more intense than the last.

When her message finally came, Mahir couldn't help but feel a mix of hope and nervousness.

Avni: Yeah, sometimes I do. It's strange, you know? We barely knew each other at school, but now... it feels different.

Mahir's heart swelled. She did feel it too. That silent pull, that unspoken connection—it wasn't just in his head.

He took a deep breath before typing his response, wanting to get the words just right.

Mahir: It does feel different. I've been thinking the same thing for a while now, but I didn't know how to bring it up.

There was a pause again, but this time it felt less tense, more expectant.

Avni: I'm glad you said it. I didn't want to be the only one feeling this way.

Mahir grinned to himself. There it was—the confirmation he had been hoping for. Avni felt it too.

He was about to reply when another message popped up from her.

Avni: But there's something else, Mahir. Something I need to tell you.

Mahir's smile faltered. What could it be? A sudden pang of worry shot through him. Was there something wrong? Did she not feel the same way after all?

Mahir: What is it? You can tell me anything.

There was an unusually long pause this time. Mahir anxiously stared at his phone, waiting, his heart thudding in his chest. When her message finally came, it was not what he expected.

Avni: My family... they've started talking about marriage. Arrange marriage.

Mahir's heart sank. The words hit him like a punch in the gut. He hadn't seen that coming, not this soon, not when things between them had just started to blossom.

Mahir: Marriage? But we're still so young...

Avni: I know. It's just talks for now, nothing serious. But they've mentioned a few prospects already.

Mahir could feel his chest tighten. This wasn't fair. Not when they were just beginning to understand each other, not when he was finally feeling close to her in a way he hadn't felt with anyone before.

Mahir: What do you think about it?

He typed the question, even though he wasn't sure if he wanted to hear the answer.

Avni's reply was swift, but it didn't give him much comfort.

Avni: Honestly? I don't know. My parents have always been traditional. They expect me to follow their lead, but... it's complicated.

Mahir: Do you want to? I mean... go along with it?

There was a brief silence before Avni answered.

Avni: Not right now, no. But I'm scared. I don't want to upset them, and they have their own expectations. I just... I don't know what to do.

Mahir could feel his pulse quicken. He had to say something, had to reassure her. The thought of her being forced into something she didn't want—something that could take her away from him—was unbearable.

Mahir: Avni, you don't have to do anything you don't want to. It's your life. You have every right to choose what makes you happy.

Avni's response was delayed, and Mahir found himself holding his breath.

Avni: I know, but it's not that easy, Mahir. I don't want to disappoint my family. It's just... I need time to figure things out.

Mahir felt a lump in his throat, but he pushed down his frustration. He didn't want to make things harder for her.

Mahir: Take your time. I'll be here, no matter what.

He sent the message, hoping it was enough. Hoping that his words gave her some kind of comfort. But deep down, Mahir couldn't shake the growing fear that time might not be on their side.

As the night wore on and their conversation slowly faded, Mahir lay on his bed, staring at the ceiling. The reality of their situation weighed heavily on him.

Avni was still here, still talking to him, still sharing her thoughts and feelings. But the looming presence of her family's expectations and the possibility of an arranged marriage threatened to pull them apart.

And Mahir knew, in his heart, that he wasn't ready to lose her. Not now. Not ever.

The Weight of Uncertainty

THE DAYS FOLLOWING Avni's revelation about her family's intentions felt different. While they still exchanged texts and talked, there was an underlying tension that neither of them could shake off. Mahir tried his best to stay positive, to continue their conversations as if nothing had changed, but it was impossible to ignore the weight that now hung over them.

One afternoon, Mahir sat at his usual spot at the local park, his favorite place to think. He often came here when he needed to clear his mind, and today was no exception. The trees swayed gently in the breeze, and the sounds of children playing in the distance felt oddly out of sync with the turmoil inside him.

He stared at his phone, hoping Avni would text him. He knew she was under pressure, but he couldn't help but wonder what she was thinking—what decision she was leaning towards. Every moment of silence from her only made him more anxious.

Finally, after what felt like an eternity, his phone buzzed. It was Avni.

Avni: Hey, can we talk?

Mahir felt his heart leap. There was something about the directness of her message that made him nervous. He quickly typed back.

Mahir: Of course. Call?

Within seconds, his phone rang. He picked it up, bracing himself for what might come next.

"Hi," Avni's voice came through the line, soft but carrying a hint of tension. "I'm sorry I haven't been able to talk much lately."

"It's okay," Mahir replied, trying to keep his tone light. "I figured you were busy."

"I've just had a lot on my mind," she said with a sigh. "About us... and my family."

Mahir clenched his jaw. He knew this was coming, but it didn't make it any easier to hear.

"I understand," he said, trying to keep his voice steady. "What are you thinking?"

There was a brief pause, and when Avni spoke again, her voice was quieter. "I've been trying to figure out what I want... and what my parents expect from me."

Mahir leaned forward, gripping the edge of the bench he was sitting on. "And?"

"I don't want to lose you," she said suddenly, her words hitting him like a punch to the chest. "But I don't know how to balance everything. My family is important to me, Mahir. They've sacrificed so much for me, and I don't want to disappoint them."

Mahir's heart ached at her words. He understood her dilemma, but the thought of losing her because of her family's expectations was unbearable.

"You don't have to choose between us," he said quietly, hoping to reassure her. "There's always a way to make both sides happy. You don't have to sacrifice one for the other."

"I wish it were that simple," Avni replied, her voice strained. "But you don't know how my family is. They've already started talking to people about potential matches, and if I tell them I want to be with someone... I don't know how they'll react."

Mahir closed his eyes, feeling the familiar surge of frustration. He hated this—hated the idea that their relationship might be dictated by someone else's rules, someone else's expectations. But more than that, he hated the thought of Avni being forced into something she didn't want.

"I can't lose you, Avni," he said softly, his voice barely above a whisper. "I... I love you."

The words hung in the air, and Mahir felt his heart pounding in his chest. It was the first time he had said it aloud, and for a moment, he wasn't sure how Avni would react.

There was silence on the other end of the line, and Mahir's stomach twisted in knots as he waited for her response. Finally, after what felt like an eternity, Avni spoke.

"I love you too, Mahir."

Relief washed over him, but it was quickly followed by a wave of uncertainty. Love, while powerful, didn't solve the problems they were facing.

"But love isn't enough," Avni continued, her voice heavy with emotion. "Not in this situation. I don't know how to make this work."

Mahir's grip on his phone tightened. He refused to accept that. There had to be a way.

"We'll figure it out," he said, determination creeping into his voice. "We'll find a way, Avni. We have to."

Avni was silent for a long moment before speaking again. "What if my parents don't accept us? What if they refuse?"

Mahir didn't have an answer for that. The truth was, he had no idea what they would do if her family said no. But he wasn't willing to give up without a fight.

"I don't know," he admitted. "But I do know that I'll be here, no matter what happens. I'll fight for us, Avni. I'll fight for you."

There was a long pause before Avni spoke again, her voice soft but resolute. "I don't want to give up either, Mahir. I don't want to lose you. But I'm scared. What if it all goes wrong?"

Mahir closed his eyes, feeling the weight of her fears pressing down on him. He didn't have all the answers, and he couldn't promise that everything would be okay. But he could promise one thing.

"We'll face it together," he said quietly. "Whatever happens, we'll face it together."

For a moment, neither of them spoke. The silence stretched between them, filled with unspoken words and shared fears. But there was also something else—something stronger. A connection, a bond that neither of them could deny.

"I just wish things were easier," Avni said finally, her voice breaking the silence.

"I know," Mahir replied softly. "But we'll make it work. We have to."

Avni sighed, and Mahir could hear the exhaustion in her voice. "I hope you're right."

"I am," he said firmly. "We'll figure it out, Avni. We'll find a way."

They continued talking for a little while longer, their conversation shifting back to lighter topics as they tried to push the heavy subject of the future aside. But even as they laughed and joked, the weight of their unspoken fears remained.

When they finally hung up, Mahir sat in silence, staring at his phone. He knew the road ahead wouldn't be easy. There were too many unknowns, too many obstacles standing in their way. But he was determined to find a way through it all.

Because, no matter what happened, he wasn't ready to let go of Avni. Not now. Not ever.

And he hoped, with everything in him, that they could face whatever came their way together.

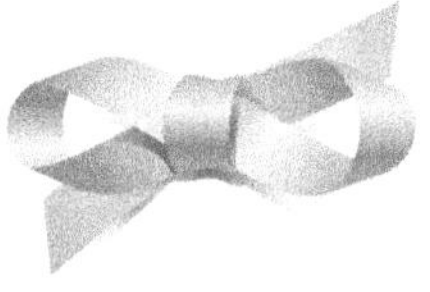

Chapter 3: Tides of Fate

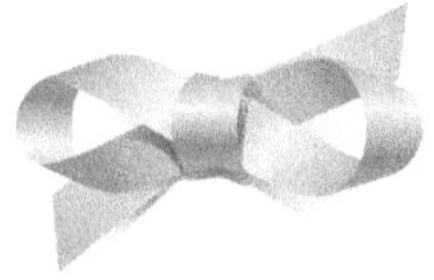

A New Horizon

THE DAYS SEEMED TO pass in a blur, a mix of hope and uncertainty clouding both Mahir and Avni's hearts. They clung to each other through late-night texts and stolen phone calls, trying to keep the reality of their situation at bay. Each message felt like a promise, a silent reassurance that they were still together, still fighting. But beneath the surface, both knew they were racing against time.

It was a Saturday afternoon when everything changed. Avni had mentioned that her parents were planning to meet a family that evening—a family who had an eligible son. The mere thought of it sent Mahir's mind spiraling, but he tried his best to stay calm. Avni had promised she wouldn't let things go too far. She reassured him that this was just a formality, something her parents insisted on, and nothing would happen without her consent.

Still, Mahir couldn't help but feel restless. The idea of her sitting across from some stranger, smiling and pretending to be interested in a future that didn't include him, gnawed at him.

As he sat in his room that afternoon, his mind wandered. What if her parents pressured her into agreeing? What if they made it impossible for her to say no? His thoughts spiraled, each scenario more terrifying than the last.

Just then, his phone buzzed. It was Avni.

Avni: They're here. Pray that this goes smoothly.

Mahir stared at the message, his heart pounding in his chest. He quickly typed back.

Mahir: I'm here with you. Whatever happens, I'm here.

He waited, staring at his phone, hoping she would reply. But minutes passed, and there was no response. He imagined her sitting in the living room with her parents, the potential groom and his family gathered around. He hated the thought of her being in that situation, but there was nothing he could do. Not yet.

Time seemed to stretch endlessly. Mahir tried to distract himself, flipping through the pages of a book, but his mind kept drifting back to Avni. His phone felt like a lifeline, the only connection he had to her in that moment. He checked it every few minutes, hoping for an update, but nothing came.

As the sun began to set, Mahir's anxiety reached its peak. He couldn't sit still any longer. He grabbed his keys and left the house, deciding to take a walk to clear his mind. The cool evening air did little to calm his nerves, but at least it gave him something to do.

He walked aimlessly, his feet carrying him through familiar streets as his mind raced. What if this was it? What if Avni came back and told him that her parents had made a decision, one she couldn't fight against? The thought made his chest tighten.

Just as he was about to turn back home, his phone buzzed. It was Avni again. His hands shook slightly as he unlocked it and read the message.

Avni: It's over. I'll call you in a bit.

That was it. No details, no explanation—just a brief message that did nothing to ease his anxiety. He felt his heart pounding in his chest as he quickly typed back.

Mahir: Are you okay? What happened?

He waited for a response, but once again, silence followed. Mahir stared at his phone, frustration building inside him. He needed to know what was going on, needed to hear her voice. He was about to call her when his phone rang. It was Avni.

"Hey," she said, her voice sounding distant and tired.

"Avni," Mahir breathed, relief flooding through him at the sound of her voice. "What happened? Are you okay?"

There was a brief pause on the other end before Avni sighed. "It was... weird. They were nice, you know? The family. But it was just so awkward. I kept thinking about you the entire time."

Mahir felt a strange mix of emotions at her words—relief that she was still thinking about him, but also frustration at the situation. "And what did your parents say?"

"They didn't say much during the meeting. Just the usual pleasantries," she explained. "But after they left, my mom started asking questions. About whether I liked the guy, what I thought of him."

Mahir's stomach twisted. "And what did you say?"

"I told her I wasn't interested," Avni replied softly. "That I didn't feel any connection with him."

Mahir let out a breath he didn't realize he was holding. "Thank God."

"But..." Avni's voice trailed off, and Mahir's heart sank.

"But what?" he asked, his voice tense.

"My dad wasn't happy," she admitted. "He thinks I'm being difficult. He said I should give it more thought, that this family is a good match and I shouldn't be so quick to dismiss them."

Mahir clenched his jaw. He had always respected Avni's family, but the idea of them pushing her into something she didn't want made his blood boil.

"And what do you think?" he asked quietly, his voice laced with worry.

"I don't know, Mahir," Avni whispered, her voice cracking slightly. "I feel like I'm being torn in two directions. I want to be with you, but I don't know how to make my parents understand that. They're so set on finding someone 'appropriate' for me. Someone from our community, someone they approve of."

Mahir's chest tightened. He had known this was coming, but hearing her say it out loud made it all too real.

"Avni, I—" He paused, unsure of what to say. He wanted to tell her that it didn't matter, that they would figure it out, but the truth was, he didn't know how they could. "We'll figure this out," he said finally, though his voice lacked the confidence he wished it had.

"I hope so," Avni replied, her voice filled with uncertainty.

They sat in silence for a few moments, neither of them knowing what to say. The weight of the situation hung heavy between them, the reality of their circumstances becoming harder to ignore with each passing day.

"I love you," Mahir said softly, breaking the silence. "I just need you to know that. No matter what happens, I love you."

Avni's breath hitched, and for a moment, he thought she might cry. "I love you too," she whispered. "I just don't know if love will be enough."

Mahir closed his eyes, the weight of her words sinking in. He wished he could make all of this go away, that he could find a way to make her family understand how much they meant to each other. But for now, all he could do was hold on to the hope that somehow, they would find a way.

As they ended the call, Mahir sat on the park bench, staring out at the fading light of the evening sky. The world around him seemed so calm, so at peace, while his own life felt like it was unraveling at the seams.

But despite the uncertainty, one thing remained clear—he wasn't ready to give up. Not yet.

A Silent Storm

THE NEXT FEW DAYS AFTER the meeting with the potential groom's family were tense. Avni's household had become a whirlwind of discussions, opinions, and subtle pressure. Though her parents hadn't outright forced her to make a decision, the weight of their expectations hung heavy on her shoulders.

Meanwhile, Mahir was caught in a storm of his own emotions. He tried to focus on his work, on his studies, but his mind kept drifting back to Avni and the uncertainty of their future. Every time his phone buzzed, his heart would leap, hoping it was her with some good news. But their conversations, though filled with love, had taken on a new edge—a quiet desperation that neither of them could fully express.

It was late on a Thursday evening when Avni called him, her voice tense.

"Mahir, we need to talk," she said, her words clipped and rushed.

Mahir's stomach dropped. "What's going on? Is everything okay?"

"No, not really," Avni admitted, her voice faltering. "My parents... they're getting serious. They want me to consider this proposal more carefully. My dad had a long conversation with me today about my future, about what's best for me."

"And what did you say?" Mahir asked, his heart pounding in his chest.

"I told them I don't want this, that I'm not interested," Avni said quickly. "But it's like they don't hear me, Mahir. They just keep talking about how 'good' this match is, how perfect it would be for me. It's like they've already made up their minds, and I'm just supposed to go along with it."

Mahir's grip tightened on his phone, frustration bubbling to the surface. "But you've already told them about us, right? About how much we love each other?"

Avni sighed, her voice laced with guilt. "I've tried, Mahir. But every time I bring you up, they brush it off. They don't take us seriously. To them, we're just a school romance, something that's not meant to last."

Mahir felt a flash of anger, his chest tightening at her words. "So, what now? What are we supposed to do?"

"I don't know," Avni whispered, her voice breaking slightly. "I'm so confused. I don't want to hurt my parents, but I can't imagine my life without you."

Her words hit Mahir like a punch to the gut. He could hear the pain in her voice, the struggle she was facing. But he also knew that they were running out of time. The more her parents pushed, the harder it would be for her to stand up against them.

"Avni, listen to me," Mahir said, his voice steady despite the storm raging inside him. "We're not just some passing fling. What we have is real. I love you, and I know you love me. We've come too far to give up now."

"I know, Mahir," Avni replied, her voice soft and full of emotion. "I know."

There was a long silence between them, the weight of the situation pressing down on both of them. Finally, Mahir spoke again.

"Do you trust me?" he asked, his voice firm.

Avni hesitated for only a moment before answering, "Yes, of course I trust you."

"Then we need to fight for this," Mahir said, determination creeping into his tone. "I know it's not easy, and I know your parents mean well, but we can't let them decide our future. We have to take control of it ourselves."

Avni took a deep breath, the resolve in Mahir's voice giving her strength. "You're right. I don't want to lose you."

"You won't," Mahir promised. "We'll figure this out, no matter what. I'm not going anywhere."

His words hung in the air like a lifeline, something for Avni to hold onto amidst the chaos surrounding her. But even as they made their promises, both knew that the road ahead would be far from easy.

That weekend, Mahir decided it was time to take matters into his own hands. He couldn't just sit back and wait for things to get worse. He needed to talk to Avni's parents, to show them that he was serious about their relationship and that he was willing to fight for her.

It was a bold move, one that could either make things better or much worse. But Mahir didn't care. He loved Avni, and he would do whatever it took to make sure they had a future together.

He called Avni the night before, laying out his plan. "I want to meet them, Avni. Your parents. I need to talk to them face-to-face."

Avni was silent for a moment, her heart racing at the thought. "Mahir, I don't know if that's a good idea. They're not exactly open to listening right now."

"I know," Mahir admitted. "But I can't just sit around and wait for them to make a decision that could ruin everything. I need to show them that I'm serious about you. About us."

"I don't want things to get worse," Avni said, her voice full of worry.

"They won't," Mahir said, though he wasn't entirely sure himself. "I'll be respectful. I'll explain how much you mean to me. Maybe if they hear it from me, they'll understand."

Avni hesitated again, but finally, she agreed. "Okay. Let's try. I just... I hope this works."

The next evening, Mahir found himself standing outside Avni's house, his heart pounding in his chest. He had dressed his best, hoping to make a good impression, but nothing could ease the nerves he felt at that moment.

Avni greeted him at the door, her face a mixture of hope and fear. "Are you sure about this?" she whispered.

Mahir nodded, though his heart was racing. "I have to do this, Avni. For us."

They walked inside, and Mahir was immediately greeted by the stern gazes of Avni's parents. Her father sat in the living room, his arms crossed over his chest, while her mother hovered nearby, her expression wary.

Mahir swallowed hard, feeling the weight of their judgment before he had even spoken a word. But he forced himself to stand tall, his resolve unwavering.

"Good evening, sir, ma'am," he began, his voice steady. "Thank you for allowing me to speak with you."

Avni's father nodded, though his expression remained hard. "What is it that you wanted to discuss, Mahir?"

Mahir took a deep breath, feeling the tension in the room. "I wanted to talk to you about Avni. About our relationship."

Her father's eyes narrowed, and Mahir could feel the weight of his disapproval. But he pressed on, refusing to back down.

"I know that you're concerned about her future, and I respect that," Mahir continued. "But I want you to know that I love her. I've loved her for a long time, and I'm willing to do whatever it takes to make her happy."

Avni's mother shifted uncomfortably, glancing at her husband. Her father remained silent for a moment before finally speaking, his voice cold.

"And what makes you think you're the right choice for our daughter?"

Mahir's heart pounded in his chest, but he didn't falter. "Because I care for her more than anything in this world. And I believe that love, real love, is worth fighting for."

Avni's parents exchanged a look, their expressions unreadable. Mahir stood there, his heart in his throat, waiting for their response.

The silence stretched on for what felt like an eternity.

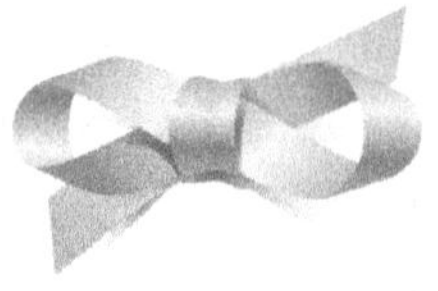

Chapter 4: The Turning Point

The Unraveling

MAHIR STOOD IN THE dimly lit living room, the tension palpable as he awaited Avni's parents' response. The silence felt like a weight pressing down on him, and he could feel Avni's anxious gaze on him, a mix of hope and fear reflected in her eyes. The atmosphere was thick with unspoken words, the kind that could change everything.

Finally, Avni's father broke the silence, his voice stern but measured. "You say you love her, Mahir. But love isn't just words. It's about responsibility, stability, and being able to provide for her future. Do you think you're ready for that?"

Mahir felt a surge of determination. He had expected this question; it was the logical next step in their conversation. "I understand your concerns, sir, and I respect them completely. But love isn't about material wealth or social status. It's about companionship, trust, and commitment. I may not have everything figured out right now, but I am determined to create a future where Avni and I can be happy together."

Avni's mother's expression softened slightly, but her father remained unyielding. "You're just a student, Mahir. What can you offer that's truly valuable? What's to say that this isn't just a phase for both of you?"

Mahir took a deep breath, feeling the weight of the scrutiny on him. "I can offer my unwavering support and my love. I will always be there for Avni, no matter what challenges we face. Love is a partnership, and I want to build that partnership with her. I want to grow with her, to face life together."

Avni's father shifted in his seat, seemingly considering Mahir's words. "And what about her education? What about her career? You know that we have plans for her future."

Mahir nodded, recognizing the importance of Avni's aspirations. "I would never ask her to give up her dreams. In fact, I want to support her in achieving them. We can help each other grow. Together, we can be strong. I believe that our love will only enhance her potential."

Avni's mother finally spoke up, her tone less confrontational. "But love isn't always enough, Mahir. There are many factors to consider when it comes to marriage. Are you ready to face the realities of life together?"

"I understand that," Mahir replied, his voice steady. "Life will throw challenges at us, but I believe we can face them together. I've seen how strong Avni is, and I know we can make it work if we have each other's backs."

Avni's father was still unconvinced, his expression tight. "You're very young, Mahir. Have you thought about what will happen if things don't work out? What if your plans fall through?"

"I believe in us," Mahir said, his voice unwavering. "I know it won't be easy, but I would rather fight for love than settle for something that doesn't make me happy. I would never want Avni to feel trapped in a situation where she isn't valued or respected. We deserve to be happy together."

Just then, Avni spoke up, her voice trembling but strong. "Dad, Mom, please. I love Mahir. I've never felt this way about anyone else. I don't want to go through life living someone else's dreams. I want to chase my own, and I want Mahir by my side."

Her words hung in the air, and Mahir felt a surge of pride at her bravery. He turned to her, his heart swelling with love. "You don't have to choose between us and your dreams. We can build a life together, where you can achieve everything you want."

The room fell silent again as Avni's parents exchanged glances. Mahir could see the uncertainty flickering in their eyes. They were torn between their love for their daughter and their protective instincts. Finally, Avni's mother spoke up again.

"Avni, sweetheart, we only want what's best for you. We've been thinking about your future and what it means for you to have stability. It's not easy for us to let go."

"I know that, Mom," Avni said softly. "But you also have to understand that I need to live my life for myself. I can't imagine a future without Mahir. Please try to see how much he means to me."

Avni's father looked thoughtful, his brow furrowed in contemplation. "It's a big decision, and we want you to think it through carefully. We're not against you being with Mahir, but we need to be sure that this is what you truly want."

Mahir felt a glimmer of hope. Perhaps this conversation was leading to a breakthrough. "I promise I will do everything in my power to prove myself to you and to take care of Avni. I want to show you that I'm serious about our future."

"But you also have to understand that this is about Avni's happiness," her father reminded him, his tone slightly softer. "We will always prioritize her well-being. That doesn't mean we want to control her life, but we need to see commitment from you."

Mahir nodded, understanding their position. "I respect that. I want you to feel secure in your daughter's happiness. I'm willing to take the time to earn your trust."

As they spoke, Mahir felt a small sense of hope beginning to blossom. The tension in the room was palpable, but he could sense a shift. Avni's parents were beginning to see his commitment, and that was a start.

But as the conversation progressed, a familiar feeling of dread began to creep back in. What if it wasn't enough? What if their parents still couldn't accept their love?

Mahir knew they had a long road ahead, and the stakes were higher than ever. Avni's parents' acceptance was crucial to their future, and he was prepared to fight for it, no matter what.

The evening wore on, and Mahir shared stories about his ambitions and dreams. He spoke about his studies, his work ethic, and the ways he planned to create a stable future for himself and Avni. With every word, he felt the barrier between them slowly begin to crumble.

Eventually, Avni's mother turned to her husband, and they exchanged another glance filled with unspoken understanding. "We'll need time to think," her father finally said, his voice softer now. "This isn't an easy decision for us, but we'll consider what you've said."

"Thank you," Mahir said, relief flooding through him. "I truly appreciate the chance to talk about this. I hope you'll see that our love is worth believing in."

After a few more minutes of conversation, Avni's parents excused themselves, leaving Mahir and Avni alone in the living room. The moment the door closed behind them, Avni rushed to Mahir, her eyes glistening with unshed tears.

"Mahir, you did it! I can't believe you stood up to them like that!" she exclaimed, a mix of excitement and fear coursing through her.

"I just told them the truth," Mahir replied, feeling a rush of adrenaline. "I meant every word."

They embraced tightly, and in that moment, Mahir felt a renewed sense of purpose. Together, they could face whatever challenges lay ahead. But deep down, he knew that this was just the beginning. The real battle for their love was still to come.

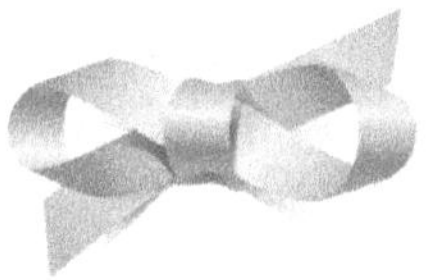

Shadows of Doubt

THE DAYS THAT FOLLOWED the conversation with Avni's parents were a whirlwind of emotions for Mahir. Hope and apprehension danced together in his mind, creating a symphony of thoughts that refused to quiet down. He and Avni were determined to make their love work, but the shadows of doubt loomed over them like dark clouds threatening to burst.

At school, the atmosphere had changed. Mahir felt a distance from his friends, who were either oblivious to his struggles or too wrapped up in their own lives to notice the storm brewing inside him. The reality of their situation weighed heavily on his shoulders. While they were all busy preparing for exams, Mahir found himself torn between academics and his commitment to Avni.

One afternoon, while sitting on a bench in the school courtyard, Mahir spotted Avni walking towards him, her usual bright smile momentarily dimmed by a look of concern. As she approached, he could see that she had been thinking deeply.

"Mahir, I've been thinking..." Avni began, her voice soft as she sat down next to him. "What if my parents don't come around? What if they never accept us?"

Mahir felt a pang in his chest. He had worried about the same thing. "I believe they will," he said, though uncertainty laced his words. "They just need time to understand how serious we are."

"But what if that time never comes?" Avni's voice quivered slightly. "What if they find someone else for me? I can't bear the thought of being forced into a marriage with someone I don't love."

Mahir reached for her hand, squeezing it gently. "No one can force you to love someone, Avni. You have a right to choose your own path, and I'll be right here with you, fighting for us."

She looked into his eyes, searching for reassurance. "Promise me you won't give up. I can't imagine a life without you."

"Promise," he said firmly, though the weight of that promise felt heavy. "I will fight for our love until my last breath."

As they sat together, the sound of laughter from nearby students filled the air, contrasting sharply with the gravity of their conversation. Mahir wished they could be carefree, lost in the bliss of young love, but reality had different plans.

Days turned into weeks, and the uncertainty of Avni's parents' decision hung like a dark cloud over them. They spent their time together studying, trying to keep their minds off the looming threat of separation. They shared stolen moments filled with laughter, but the shadows of doubt continued to creep in, tainting their happiness.

One evening, as they walked home from school, Avni suddenly stopped. "Mahir, what if I told my parents that I want to take some time away from everything? Just to think?"

Mahir frowned, concern etched on his face. "Are you sure that's a good idea? They might see it as a rebellion."

"But I need space to think about us, about my life," Avni insisted, her voice rising slightly. "I can't keep pretending everything is okay when I feel so trapped."

Mahir could see her frustration boiling over, and it made his heart ache. He wanted to support her, but he also worried about the consequences. "I understand you need time, but we should approach this carefully. We can't risk losing their support completely."

Avni sighed, her shoulders slumping in defeat. "I just feel so overwhelmed. My parents have always had plans for me, and now I don't know how to tell them that I want something different."

Mahir stepped closer, wrapping his arms around her shoulders. "We'll figure this out together. Just remember, I'm here for you. No matter what."

As the days continued to pass, Mahir noticed a change in Avni. The spark that usually lit up her eyes was dimming, replaced by a constant look of worry. He could tell she was wrestling with her feelings, and it was breaking his heart to see her like this.

One afternoon, as they sat in their favorite café, Avni's phone buzzed on the table. She glanced at it, and her expression shifted. "It's my mom," she said, her voice trembling.

"Answer it," Mahir urged, sensing the tension in the air. "Maybe they've come to a decision."

Avni hesitated, biting her lip before picking up the phone. She took a deep breath and pressed the answer button. "Hi, Mom..."

Mahir watched her closely, the uncertainty knotting in his stomach. Avni's face changed as her mother spoke, her brow furrowing with concern. "What's happening?" he whispered when she hung up.

Avni looked devastated, her eyes glistening with unshed tears. "They want to meet... and they're bringing someone with them," she choked out, her voice barely above a whisper.

Mahir's heart sank. "What do you mean, someone?"

"They're trying to set me up with a guy," she said, her voice cracking. "They don't think you're serious enough for me."

Mahir felt the ground shift beneath him. "No... No, Avni, they can't do that. You have to tell them you don't want it!"

"I can't just defy them like that!" she cried, tears streaming down her cheeks. "They'll never forgive me! I can't lose my family."

Mahir wiped her tears gently with his thumb, feeling helpless. "But you can't lose yourself either. You can't let them dictate who you should love."

Avni looked up at him, her eyes filled with anguish. "I don't know what to do, Mahir! I feel like I'm being torn apart."

The weight of the moment pressed heavily on Mahir's chest. He had always wanted to be her rock, but right now, he felt equally lost. "No matter what happens, I'll always be here for you. You're not alone in this."

As Avni leaned into him, they both knew that the coming days would be crucial. Their love was being tested, and they would have to find the strength to fight for it, no matter the cost.

That night, as Mahir lay in bed, he couldn't shake the feeling of dread. The shadows of doubt loomed larger than ever, threatening to engulf them both. The love he felt for Avni was unwavering, but the world around them was unpredictable and dangerous.

He needed a plan, a way to show her parents that he was serious and capable of providing a future for Avni. It was clear that words alone wouldn't be enough; he needed to take action. He needed to prove that their love was worth fighting for.

With resolve hardening in his heart, Mahir began to formulate a plan. It wouldn't be easy, but he was willing to do whatever it took to protect their love, even if it meant stepping into a world that was dark and uncertain.

Chapter 5: The Unbreakable Bond

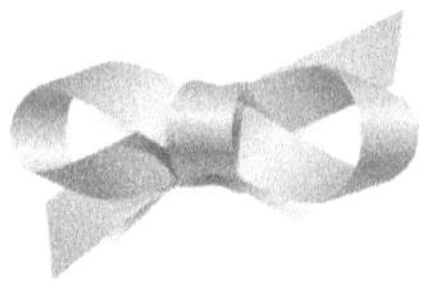

Rising Tensions

MAHIR STOOD IN FRONT of the mirror, adjusting his tie for what felt like the hundredth time. Today was a pivotal day—a day that could either strengthen his bond with Avni or shatter it into pieces. He had spent the night brainstorming ways to impress her parents, but now, as he prepared to meet them, anxiety coiled tightly around his chest.

"Just breathe," he whispered to himself, trying to shake off the nerves. He thought about Avni and the love they had built over the past months. He remembered her laughter, the warmth of her smile, and the moments they shared, all of which fueled his determination to fight for their love.

The plan was simple: show her parents that he was not just a schoolboy in love but a young man ready to take responsibility. He had arranged to meet them at a nearby café, a neutral ground where he could introduce himself without the heaviness of their home looming over them. With one last deep breath, Mahir grabbed his phone and sent Avni a quick text.

"I'm on my way. Remember, no matter what happens, I love you."

As he stepped out of his house, Mahir felt the weight of his promise to Avni settle on his shoulders. He knew she was anxious too; the phone call from her mother had left her reeling, and the uncertainty of the meeting gnawed at her. He needed to be her rock today.

When he arrived at the café, Mahir spotted Avni seated at a table, her fingers nervously fidgeting with the hem of her sweater. She looked beautiful, but he could see the worry etched on her face. As he approached, her eyes lit up momentarily, but the tension returned as she glanced past him, searching for her parents.

"Mahir, I'm so glad you're here," she whispered, relief washing over her features.

"Hey, we'll get through this together," he assured her, squeezing her hand. "Just remember, I'm serious about us."

Avni nodded, but her eyes betrayed her fear. "What if they don't like you? What if they don't see how much I care for you?"

"They will," Mahir said confidently. "Just trust me, okay? I've got a plan."

Just then, Avni's parents walked in, and the atmosphere shifted. Mr. and Mrs. Malhotra appeared stern, their expressions unreadable as they scanned the café. Mahir stood up, straightening his back, determined to present himself as composed and mature.

"Good afternoon, Mr. and Mrs. Malhotra," he greeted, forcing a smile. "Thank you for agreeing to meet with me."

Mrs. Malhotra's gaze bore into him, her scrutiny evident. "We're here because Avni insisted, but I hope you understand that this is a serious conversation."

Mahir nodded, feeling the weight of their expectations. "Of course, I understand. I respect your concern for Avni's future."

They sat down, the tension palpable. Mahir glanced at Avni, who was anxiously biting her lip. He could sense her need for reassurance and knew he had to keep the conversation focused and respectful.

Mr. Malhotra leaned forward, folding his hands on the table. "Let's cut to the chase. Why should we believe that you are a suitable match for our daughter?"

Mahir swallowed hard but maintained eye contact. "I understand that I am young, but I am deeply in love with Avni. I have been focused on my studies, and I have goals for my future. I plan to pursue a career that will allow me to support her."

Mrs. Malhotra raised an eyebrow. "And what makes you think you can provide for her? You're still in school."

"I know I am, ma'am," Mahir replied, his heart racing. "But I am also building my own path. I've started a small business that I hope will grow. I want to prove to you that I can be responsible and successful."

Avni's parents exchanged glances, their expressions softening slightly, but skepticism still lingered. Mahir knew he needed to dig deeper. "I care for Avni more than anything. I want her to be happy, and I will always support her dreams. That is my promise."

Mrs. Malhotra folded her arms, still unsure. "But what about your future? What are your plans after school? What if things don't work out?"

Mahir's mind raced as he considered how to convey his determination. "I've thought about that a lot. I plan to pursue a degree in business and expand my ventures. But more importantly, I want to be someone Avni can rely on. I don't want her to feel trapped in a marriage she doesn't want."

Mr. Malhotra shifted in his seat, clearly contemplating Mahir's words. "You speak well, but love isn't always enough. It requires stability and maturity, qualities that come with time."

Mahir nodded, acknowledging the truth in his statement. "I understand that, sir. But I believe that love can be the foundation on which we build our lives. Avni and I can face the challenges together."

The conversation shifted as Avni finally found her voice. "Mom, Dad, I know this is difficult for you, but please understand that I want to make my own choices. I love Mahir, and he makes me happy. I can't imagine my life without him."

Her parents looked taken aback, clearly surprised by Avni's boldness. Mahir could see the fear in her eyes, but he also felt a surge of pride at her courage. This was the moment when they would stand together, united against the world.

Mrs. Malhotra sighed deeply, rubbing her temples. "Avni, we just want what's best for you. We've always had plans for your future."

"I know," Avni replied, her voice steady. "But I need you to see that my happiness matters too. I want to make my own choices and follow my heart."

Mr. Malhotra remained silent, contemplating the weight of his daughter's words. Mahir could feel the atmosphere shift slightly, the tension loosening just a bit.

As they spoke, Mahir felt a surge of hope. Maybe they were getting through to her parents. He wanted to believe that love could overcome all obstacles, and he was determined to prove it.

After what felt like hours of conversation, Mrs. Malhotra finally spoke. "We need time to think about this, Avni. It's not an easy decision for us, but we appreciate your honesty."

Mahir felt a mixture of relief and anxiety wash over him. They hadn't outright rejected him, but the road ahead was still fraught with uncertainty. "Thank you for considering my feelings," he said sincerely. "I truly care for Avni, and I'm willing to do whatever it takes to prove it."

As the meeting drew to a close, Mahir looked at Avni, and for a moment, time stood still. In that shared glance, he saw a flicker of hope. They were in this together, no matter the outcome.

Once they exited the café, Avni turned to Mahir, her eyes shimmering with tears. "What if they still don't accept you?"

"Then we'll find another way," Mahir promised, pulling her into a comforting embrace. "We'll face whatever comes next, together."

Avni buried her face in his shoulder, and Mahir held her tightly, knowing that this was only the beginning of their journey. The challenges ahead would test their love, but he was ready to fight for her, to prove that their bond was unbreakable.

As they walked away from the café, hand in hand, Mahir felt a renewed sense of determination. Love had brought them this far, and he would not let anything come between them. Whatever lay ahead, they would face it together, united in their dreams and unwavering in their commitment.

The Wedding Dream

DAYS TURNED INTO WEEKS as Mahir and Avni waited anxiously for her parents to make a decision. The uncertainty hung heavily in the air, but their bond grew stronger with each passing day. They navigated the ups and downs together, finding solace in their shared dreams of a future that seemed both distant and close at the same time.

One evening, as they strolled through the park, the sun dipped below the horizon, painting the sky in shades of orange and purple. Mahir glanced at Avni, who was lost in thought. He could see the flicker of worry in her eyes, and he knew he had to lift her spirits.

"Hey, what are you thinking about?" he asked, nudging her gently.

Avni looked up, a small smile breaking through her pensive expression. "I was just imagining what our wedding would be like. You know, the kind of wedding where everything feels magical."

Mahir felt his heart skip a beat at her words. The idea of marrying Avni had always filled him with a sense of joy and excitement, but hearing her talk about it made it feel so much more real. "Tell me more about your dream wedding," he urged, wanting to explore this beautiful vision with her.

"Well, I picture a beautiful garden filled with flowers," Avni began, her eyes sparkling with enthusiasm. "We'd have fairy lights strung across the trees, and our friends and family would be there to celebrate with us."

Mahir nodded, captivated by her description. "What kind of dress do you see yourself in?"

"I imagine wearing a flowing white gown with delicate lace and a long train," she replied, twirling around playfully, the wind catching her hair. "And I want you in a sharp suit, looking handsome as ever."

He chuckled, his heart swelling with affection. "I'll do my best to look dashing, just for you."

As they continued to share their dreams, the worries that had weighed heavily on their shoulders began to fade. The laughter and joy they exchanged created a bubble of happiness, a brief escape from the reality they faced.

But as they walked home that night, a sense of foreboding crept back in. The next day would mark the moment of truth. Avni's parents had finally agreed to meet Mahir again, and the stakes felt higher than ever.

The following afternoon, they found themselves back at the café, a familiar tension hanging in the air. Avni's parents arrived, their expressions still cautious but a hint of curiosity glimmering in their eyes. Mahir could feel his heart racing, but he remained determined.

"Thank you for meeting with us again," he said, standing tall as they greeted him. "I appreciate this opportunity."

Mr. Malhotra wasted no time. "We've discussed your proposal, Mahir, and we still have reservations. But we want to understand your intentions better."

Avni reached for Mahir's hand, squeezing it tightly for support. He took a deep breath, knowing this was his chance to make them see the depth of his love for their daughter.

"I love Avni more than anything," he began, looking directly at her parents. "I want to build a future with her, filled with love, trust, and respect. I know I'm still young, but I'm committed to working hard to create a life that fulfills both of our dreams."

Mrs. Malhotra leaned forward, her curiosity piqued. "And what about your plans for the future? Can you guarantee stability?"

"Yes, ma'am. I've been working on my business, and I'm dedicated to growing it. I want to provide for Avni, not just financially but emotionally. I want her to feel secure and loved."

Mr. Malhotra exchanged glances with his wife, and for a moment, Mahir saw a flicker of understanding in their eyes. "You seem sincere, but love is just one part of marriage. It requires mutual respect and compatibility."

"I completely agree, sir," Mahir replied earnestly. "Avni and I complement each other in ways that make us stronger together. We share our dreams, support each other's ambitions, and most importantly, we respect one another."

Avni smiled at him, her eyes shining with pride. It was a small gesture, but it filled him with warmth and resolve. They had come too far to let fear dictate their future.

After a brief pause, Mr. Malhotra continued, "If we are to consider this, we need to see you both committed to your futures. You will need to prove that you can stand on your own and support Avni in her goals."

Mahir nodded, grateful for the chance. "I'm ready to do whatever it takes. Avni's happiness is my priority, and I will work hard to earn your trust."

Mrs. Malhotra smiled softly, "And Avni, are you certain about your feelings for Mahir? This decision will affect your life in many ways."

Avni took a deep breath, her heart racing. "I am certain, Mom. I love Mahir, and I believe in us. I want to build my future with him. Please give us a chance to prove that love can conquer all."

The conversation shifted as they explored the realities of their relationship, discussing their dreams, aspirations, and how they planned to navigate life together. Mahir felt a sense of hope growing in the room, fueled by their honesty and vulnerability.

As the meeting drew to a close, Avni's parents shared a look of contemplation. "We will discuss this further," Mr. Malhotra said, his tone more open than before. "You both deserve the chance to explore your feelings, but remember that the path ahead will not be easy."

Mahir felt a rush of gratitude as they left the café, a flicker of optimism igniting in his heart. "I think they're starting to come around," he said, glancing at Avni, who looked hopeful.

"I hope so," she replied, squeezing his hand. "Thank you for being there for me. I couldn't have done this without you."

They walked side by side, the weight of uncertainty still present, but their hearts were filled with a shared dream—one that shimmered like the stars above. The idea of their wedding lingered in the air, a promise of a future they both yearned for.

In that moment, Mahir knew that love was a journey, and together, they would face whatever challenges lay ahead. With determination and unwavering support for one another, they were ready to build the life they dreamed of—a life woven with love, laughter, and an unbreakable bond.

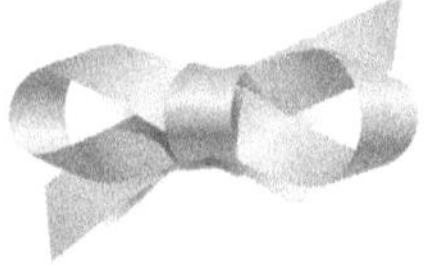

The End!!